This book belongs to:

_____

Digital art by Callaway Animation Studios under the direction of David Kirk in collaboration with Nelvana Limited.

This book is based on the TV episode "Basketberry Blues," written by Elizabeth Keyishian and David Wilks, from
the animated TV series *Miss Spider's Sunny Patch Friends* on Nick Jr., a Nelvana Limited/Absolute Pictures Limited
co-production in association with Callaway Arts & Entertainment, based on the Miss Spider books by David Kirk.

Nicholas Callaway, President and Publisher
Cathy Ferrara, Managing Editor and Production Director
Toshiya Masuda, Art Director • Nelson Gomez, Director of Digital Services
Joya Rajadhyaksha, Associate Editor • Amy Cloud, Associate Editor
Bill Burg, Digital Artist • Keith McMenamy, Digital Artist • Christina Pagano, Digital Artist
Raphael Shea, Art Assistant • Krupa Jhaveri, Design Assistant

Special thanks to the Nelvana staff, including Doug Murphy, Scott Dyer, Tracy Ewing, Pam Lehn,
Tonya Lindo, Mark Picard, Susie Grondin, Luis Lopez, Eric Pentz, and Georgina Robinson.

Library of Congress Cataloging-in-Publication Data available upon request.

Distributed in the United States by Penguin Young Readers Group.

Callaway Arts & Entertainment, its Callaway logotype,
and Callaway & Kirk Company LLC are trademarks.

978-0-448-45009-4

Visit Callaway Arts & Entertainment at www.callaway.com.

10 9 8 7 6 5 4 3 2 1   08 09 10

Printed in China

Miss Spider's SUNNY PATCH FRIENDS

Basketberry Blues

David Kirk

CALLAWAY

NEW YORK

2008

The Sunny Patch kids were practicing basketberry before the Taddy Puddler team tryouts.

Dragon dunked the ball through the hoop.

"Dragon's team wins!" said Spinner.

"Hey, my little basketberry superstars," Miss Spider called. "Time to come home and help with dinner!"

"I'm no superstar," Spinner said. "That's why I keep score."

Later, Miss Spider told Dragon, "I think Spinner would like to learn how to play basketberry. A spiderific player like you would be the perfect coach!"

"You're right!" Dragon replied. "I bet I could help him get some game!"

Dragon tried to teach Spinner how to play. But every time Spinner threw the ball at the hoop, it flew in another direction.

"See, Dragon? I'm just no good," Spinner said sadly.

Squirt came to watch them.

"Spinner would feel better if he could just make one basket," he told Dragon.

"I have an idea. Can you spin a web thread that is hard to see?" Dragon asked.

"Sure," Squirt replied.

"Then let's help Spinner make a basket!"

"Spinner, why don't you try to relax? Take off your glasses," Dragon suggested.

He handed Spinner a new ball with a very thin web thread attached.

"Now, just think *swish!*" he told him.

"Buggin' shot, Spinner!"
Dragon cheered.

"I can't believe it went in!" yelled
Spinner happily.

Without his glasses, Spinner
could not see that Squirt had
pulled the ball through the hoop.

At dinner, Spinner beamed. "You should have seen my shot, Mom! I'm going to be the superstar of the Taddy Puddlers! Right, Coach?"

"Um . . . right," Dragon replied, sounding unsure.

Later that evening, Bounce said, "Did you see Spinner's shots? *Wow!*"

"But Bounce," Dragon replied, "he didn't make those baskets. We tied a web thread around the ball, and Squirt pulled it through the hoop."

Spinner appeared in the doorway. "You pulled the ball through the hoop?" he asked.

"Sorry, Spinner," said Squirt. "We were just trying to help."

"I know you meant well, but it was not a good idea to fool Spinner," Miss Spider told Dragon.

"He's just not very good, Mom," Dragon said.

"It's not important how good you are," Miss Spider replied. "It's important how much fun you have!"

The big day arrived, but Spinner refused to try out.

"I'm your coach," Dragon told him. "And I say, it doesn't matter how good you are. It's more important that you have fun!"

Spinner decided to give it a try.

Spinner's heart was pounding as he stepped up to the basket. But then he remembered how much fun he had practicing with Dragon, and he felt better.

Spinner threw the ball. It danced on the edge of the hoop, rolled around the rim, and then . . .

It went in the basket!

"You can be on the team!" said Coach Grub.

"I can't believe I made the Taddy Puddlers!" Spinner laughed.

Everybuggy cheered as they lifted Spinner in the air.